The K...
Injured Tail

"She will be all right, won't she, Dad?"

"I'll be honest, Emma, I really can't say. She's weak and *very* young – it could go either way at this stage. I'm going to put them all under infrared lights, and place a sheepskin blanket beneath them. It's so important to keep them warm."

When the kittens were settled, Emma plodded reluctantly up the stairs to read. But Tiny, with her injured tail and frail little body, kept popping into her mind and she found it difficult to concentrate.

The Kitten with the Injured Tail

Brenda Jobling

SCHOLASTIC

Scholastic Children's Books,
Commonwealth House, 1-19 New Oxford Street,
London WC1A 1NU, UK
A division of Scholastic Ltd
London ~ New York ~ Toronto ~ Sydney ~ Auckland
Mexico City ~ New Delhi ~ Hong Kong

First published by Scholastic Ltd, 2000

Text copyright © Brenda Jobling, 2000
Cover illustration copyright © Jacques Fabre, 2000

ISBN 0 439 01180 9

Typeset by
Cambrian Typesetters, Frimley, Camberley, Surrey
Printed by
Norhaven Paperback, Denmark

10 9 8 7 6 5

For Janey with her many cats – and Cynthia and Ian who took in the little, stray, mother cat and her litter of kittens.

Chapter 1

"Did you say you'd found a box full of *kittens*, Mrs Higgins?"

"Yes, that's right, dear, kittens! A whole box of them, just lying among the rubbish in the alleyway. I found them when I went to my bin," replied the old lady's excited voice at the end of the telephone.

"Just how many kittens did you see?"

"Well – I didn't actually *see* any, dear, but I *heard* mewing sounds coming from inside the box."

Emma felt puzzled, but satisfied that Mrs Higgins had stumbled across some sort of animal life.

"Thank you for letting us know, Mrs

1

Higgins. We'll look into it straight away," she said, eager to find out more about the contents of the box.

Emma Hodges was fourteen. She was the daughter of a busy veterinary surgeon, Christopher Hodges, who owned and ran Handley Road Veterinary Clinic from a big old house in North London. The clinic occupied the ground floor and Emma and her family lived in the upper floors. Emma loved living there – so close to animals.

Ever since she could remember, it had been her dream to work as a vet in her father's practice. When she was small she had pretended her soft, fluffy, toy animals were patients and had carefully treated and bandaged them. Now she was older, her father let her help out in the clinic on Saturday mornings. It was her job to show the animals and their owners into the surgery.

Although Emma didn't assist in any procedures, she was allowed to stay and watch. She had a good memory. At night, before going to sleep, she made notes about the methods her father used to treat different patients. She hoped the notes would come in useful when she went to veterinary college. Emma felt very determined about that. Jack, her brother, was already there. When he came home for holidays he helped out in the busy surgery.

"Jamie!" Emma called, rushing from room to room in the clinic, looking for the sixteen-year-old boy who worked for her father by doing all sorts of odd jobs. As she turned a corner, she almost collided with him outside the surgery. He was carrying a huge bag of dog biscuits.

"I've just had a call from Mrs Higgins," Emma panted. "She said there's a box of kittens in the alleyway behind her flats. Is there any chance you could spare some time to take a look with me?"

"Let's go!" answered Jamie by way of a reply, as he hurriedly stacked the dog biscuits on a display in reception.

"Where are you two going?" asked Sue, the friendly receptionist.

"Mrs Higgins phoned," Emma explained. "She seems to think there are some kittens in the alleyway. We're going to investigate."

"Now why is it that I get a strong feeling the kittens will end up here, if you have anything to do with them, Emma?"

Sue smiled and stroked her dog, Old Vic. He raised one floppy eyelid and peered sleepily at her. Giving a great sigh, his rubbery jaws fell over his paws and he returned to sleep.

"Perhaps you'd let Dad know where I am when he comes out of his surgery," said Emma.

"As long as you ask your dad before you decide to adopt a family of kittens," Sue called after her. "They're probably wild, feral cats and quite happy living there."

The alleyway was narrow, damp and smelled to Emma of rotting vegetables.

"Ugh! Jamie, it stinks around here. Look at all that discarded rubbish lying on the ground. It hasn't even been put in the bins." She clasped one hand over her nose.

"Well, if there *are* kittens, I would imagine they'll have plenty of rats and mice to eat when they get older," Jamie replied.

"If there *are* kittens, don't think I'm going to leave them abandoned here," said Emma, stepping aside to avoid a mushy lump of bread.

They padded quietly along the alleyway, to the spot where Mrs Higgins had told Emma the box lay in a pile of rubbish.

"Hey, look!" said Emma, pointing to a battered cardboard box near some overfilled bins. "Do you think the kittens could be in there?"

"Well there's one way to find out," Jamie answered as he crept towards it.

"Can you see anything?" asked Emma impatiently.

Carefully lifting the lid, Jamie peered inside. "Just a load of empty tin cans." He continued searching in the rubbish, while Emma wandered further down the alleyway.

"Jamie!" she suddenly called. "Quick! See that little box by the stack of old newspapers? Well – just listen and watch it move."

They watched the box shake and heard gentle high-pitched mews drifting out.

"Mrs Higgins has got to be right – that's definitely kittens," said Emma. "Let's take it slowly; we don't want to frighten them."

As Emma and Jamie crept forwards, a small, bedraggled, black cat startled them. It jumped from a wall and headed quickly towards the box.

"Perhaps it's their mother," whispered Emma. "She looks in bad condition. I'm pretty sure she's not a feral cat though."

Emma watched the bony-looking cat warily push aside the flaps and squeeze inside the box without making a sound.

"Listen to the mewing now," she whispered as the box wobbled with increased movement. "It *must* be their mum, poor thing. She's probably come back to feed her litter so I don't think we should disturb them."

"It's best to get your dad to take a look," suggested Jamie.

"Agreed. If you keep watch, I'll creep off and see if he's finished his surgery yet."

Emma stood up and brushed away some potato peelings that had stuck to her jeans, and Jamie settled to watch for further activity from the box.

"I hope you're not too long. It's really beginning to whiff around here," he grimaced.

"I'd better take a wire basket," said Mr Hodges. "I think we should fetch the mother cat and her litter back here to check them over. You said she looked really scrawny and nervous – so we must take care not to frighten her away."

"I wonder how they got there?" said Emma.

"Well – they could have been abandoned by someone who just didn't want the bother of finding homes for the kittens. Or they may well have been born in the alleyway. If that's the case, then the young mother cat has probably been foraging in the rubbish for food. She needs to sustain herself, so she can feed her litter."

*   *   *

Emma and her father carried the metal transporter along the alleyway until they reached Jamie. He was crouching low, still keeping a close watch on the box.

"Anything happened while I was gone?" whispered Emma.

"Nothing to report, except I think the kittens have finished feeding. There hasn't been as much as a mew for at least five minutes."

"Right, what we need to do," said Mr Hodges thoughtfully, "is to manoeuvre the cardboard box carefully into the transporter."

"If you put the basket behind the box," suggested Jamie, "I think I could ease it in from behind."

"Good idea," said Mr Hodges.

He opened the big wire cage. Taking great care not to disturb the contents, Jamie carefully slid the box into the transporter and Mr Hodges fastened it shut.

"Oh, look Dad, the mother cat has poked her head out. She has the sweetest face," Emma cooed.

Two pale green eyes stared nervously at

the faces peering in, before the cat quickly disappeared back inside the box.

"She's definitely a young one," Mr Hodges observed.

Emma walked in front of her father and Jamie as they carried the transporter between them. Free of the alleyway, they took deep breaths, drawing the fresh air deep into their lungs.

Emma could hardly wait to see inside the cardboard box, as Jamie and her father lifted it on to the big rubber-topped table in the surgery. As the flaps were opened and the contents were revealed, she caught her breath.

Chapter 2

"Oh, just look at them! They're adorable – and so tiny!" Emma tried hard to contain her excitement. "I can count three of them, but they're snuggled up so close, it's difficult to see where one ends and the other begins."

"They can't be much over a week old," said Mr Hodges. "Their eyes are still closed. Kittens usually have them open by about the tenth day. Their mother looks barely a year herself."

Emma stared down at the delicate little creatures. She noticed that although they were awake, their movements were sleepy and clumsy; tiny paws and legs stretched, then flopped across each other's faces. She watched the rise and fall of the kittens' tummies as they breathed, and studied the features of each one as it attempted to wriggle closer to its mother.

"From what I can see there is one entirely black kitten, like its mother; one black with a few white markings, and another black kitten with four white paws." She peered more closely and gasped as another kitten emerged from beneath the others. "Oh my goodness! There are *four* of them. A tortoiseshell has just appeared."

Emma felt herself melting when she looked at the kitten. "Look, Jamie – it's so beautiful! Didn't you tell me tortoiseshells are always female, Dad?"

"That's right," said Mr Hodges, watching the minute bundle of mottled brown fur.

"I wonder if there are any other girls in the litter," said Emma.

"Well, we'll take a good look at each of them when they've had time to settle after the move. Their mother, especially, needs some attention. She's a sorry sight – and

11

extremely nervous. Poor creature looks half-starved herself, let alone able to provide nourishment for her kittens."

The mother cat heard the faint squeak of the door closing as Mr Hodges, Emma and Jamie left the room. She felt confused lying in a strange room with her young ones gathered around her.

"Right, I think it's about time to check the condition of this little family," said Mr Hodges, entering the room with Emma, an hour later.

Emma looked at the mother cat, lying just as they had left her, with the four little kittens snuggled close to her side. Mr Hodges reached in to lift her out, immediately aware of her scrawny body tensing up with fear.

"Look at her, Dad. She's petrified."

"I want you to try and hold her steady while I examine her," said Mr Hodges. He placed the cat on the large rubber-topped table. "She might struggle a bit, but if you get a firm hold, the way I've shown you, I don't think she'll scratch."

"Gently but firmly – that's how I need to hold you," Emma thought, watching her father run his hands over the cat's stick-like limbs. To Emma's amazement, she didn't attempt to struggle.

Mr Hodges cradled her head in one hand and examined both eyes. Then, carefully prising open her mouth, he looked inside.

"As far as I can see she isn't suffering from any particular complaint, but she is undernourished. She needs building up – plenty of fresh food and vitamins," he said. He placed the cat back in the box and lifted out one of the kittens.

"Now this little fellow appears to be in better shape," he said, examining the kitten. The ball of black fur fitted snugly in his hand.

"This one isn't too bad either," he continued, taking another of the kittens from the box. "And – it's another male."

"Oh, Dad, they're all so sweet."

Mr Hodges put the two kittens next to their mother and reached in to lift out a third one.

"Is *that* one a girl?" Emma eagerly enquired.

"No, Em, another male. He's a little sticky around the eyes, but apart from that seems to be in much the same condition as the others."

"I love his four little white paws – just like ankle-socks," Emma giggled.

As Mr Hodges removed the remaining kitten, Emma caught her breath when she saw the tiny tortoiseshell again.

"My favourite," she gasped.

"Yes, the only female in the litter," said Mr Hodges. "I'm afraid she's the only really weak one, too."

Emma stroked the top of the beautiful little kitten's head with her forefinger. "She will be all right, won't she, Dad?"

"I hope so. There's often one weak kitten in a litter. The best thing we can do is to make them as comfortable and as warm as possible in one of the rooms off the surgery. We'll feed the mother nutritious food, and watch them at regular intervals."

Emma watched her father place the kitten next to her mother and brothers again. She noticed that, although they were all small, the tortoiseshell was half the size of the other kittens.

She decided to take her mind off worrying about her favourite kitten by organizing bedding and feeding areas inside a pen. It lay in a small room near the surgery.

"I'll make everything as snug as possible," she thought, placing down bowls for the mother cat's food and water.

"That looks lovely and cosy," said Mr Hodges, carrying the box with the mother cat and her kittens into the room. "I could almost crawl in and nod off to sleep," he laughed.

He lifted the mother cat out of the box and placed her inside the pen.

"She's very wary," Emma remarked. "See how she's sniffing around."

"That's pretty normal," replied Mr Hodges. "Once they're all in, we should leave them alone again. She'll need to get used to her new environment."

He crouched down ready for Emma to hand him the kittens.

"I know you don't think it's a good idea to get too attached to the animals that come into the clinic, but I'd love to give the kittens names. It's just as a way of telling one from the other," suggested Emma.

Mr Hodges smiled, then nodded in agreement. As she passed him the all-black kitten first, Emma looked thoughtfully at the little sleepy face.

"I shall call this one Midnight," she said. "And this one –" she paused for a moment, lifting another curled up kitten from the box – "I'll call you Shadow. You're as dark as Midnight, but you've got a few little white patches on your face and tummy."

As she lifted the last male into her father's waiting hands she announced: "Now you – dear little thing – I'll call you Socks because of your four lovely white paws."

The kitten wriggled feebly as he was placed inside.

Emma took care to cradle her favourite kitten in her hands. "Until I can think of something more fitting, I'll call you – Tiny."

She felt how fragile Tiny seemed compared with her brothers. "I *do* hope you get stronger – and it had better be very soon, by the look of you."

The mother cat padded down the soft towelling Emma had placed in the pen, arranging it just the way she wanted it. Lifting her kittens by the scruff of loose fur on the back of their necks, she shifted them around before settling to feed again.

"What a busy life you mother cats have," Emma smiled.

Emma lay in bed that night thinking about the young mother cat and her precious kittens, especially Tiny.

"I wish I could snuggle you next to me," she thought, eventually drifting off to sleep. "At least it's Saturday tomorrow. I'll be helping out at the clinic, so there will be lots of opportunities to visit you."

Downstairs in their snug, warm pen the kittens lay huddled close to their mother. She found the clean, quiet room very different from the alleyway and raised her head at the slightest sound. She looked at her kittens as they slept, aware of the warmth and comfort she gave them.

Chapter 3

" *The kittens! Tiny!*" Emma jumped out of bed on Saturday morning and made a dash for the bathroom. "I'd better hurry up and see how they're doing."

She washed and dressed hurriedly before racing downstairs. Carefully opening the door to the room where the kittens were housed, she was surprised to find her father and Jamie already there.

"We've put fresh food down for the mother cat," announced Mr Hodges. "We'll leave their bedding – best not to disturb them any more than necessary at the moment. They seem pretty much the same as yesterday. The mother and Tiny are the ones needing most attention. Tiny doesn't appear to be feeding."

"Look at the other greedy kittens. Socks, Midnight and Shadow are guzzling away. I don't think Tiny would stand much of a chance even if she *was* hungry," said Emma.

"We should start to see an improvement in the mother if she keeps eating regularly," said Mr Hodges. "So we need to do everything we can to encourage her. Let's make sure it's kept as quiet as possible out here. We can try to feed Tiny by other methods, if necessary, but I'd like to give her a bit longer with her mother. Her milk is what Tiny needs to build her up."

The sudden insistent ringing of the doorbell startled everyone.

"That will be Casey," smiled Mr Hodges. "One of his hamsters is my first patient this morning. Perhaps you'd like to show him into the surgery, Emma."

"Right, Dad," she said, taking one last look at Tiny, who was still fast asleep. "Come *on*, Tiny," she whispered, feeling sad at seeing her favourite kitten sleeping while her brothers fed. "*Please* wake up and feed."

"Hi, Mr Hodges," said the small boy striding into the vet's surgery, grasping a wooden box with crude air holes pierced in the lid.

"Which one have you brought today?" Mr Hodges invited Casey to place the box on the rubber-topped table.

"Hercules!" announced Emma, reading from the animal's report card, before Casey had a chance to reply. "A four-year-old golden hamster."

"He's got a lump on his side, and it's not one of his pouches full up with food – I've checked," said Casey, lifting the little tan-coloured creature out of the box.

He placed Hercules in the middle of the big table. The hamster sat twitching his whiskers and grooming himself, rubbing behind his ears with his paws.

Mr Hodges let Hercules run around while he observed him. "Let's take a closer look at this fine specimen," he said after a minute, gently lifting the hamster into his palm.

He felt the little creature all over, nodding as his fingers made contact with a tiny lump on Hercules' side.

"Well spotted, Casey. It's nothing serious, but I think it would be a good idea to remove it. Don't worry. Just bring Hercules in on Monday morning and I'll operate on him then."

"Operate!" said Casey, taken aback. "Will you have to give him an anaesthetic? Will he be out for days, recovering?"

"Slow down, Casey. It's not an emergency; there's no need to panic. You should be able to collect Hercules on the same day as his operation," smiled the vet, placing the hamster back on the table. He watched him scuttle off, stopping to twitch and sniff every few steps before setting off in another direction to explore.

Emma showed Casey out of the surgery. She could see he still looked worried about Hercules.

"How would you like to see a young mother cat and her four kittens?" she whispered in his ear to cheer him up.

"Yes, please," said Casey.

"You'll have to stay very quiet near the kittens. Their mother is nervous. We must be careful not to frighten her," Emma warned as he followed her.

"They're lovely – as small as Hercules!" Casey gasped, peering into the pen. "Oh, *please* can I hold one of them?"

"I'm afraid not," answered Emma. "They're still very fragile."

The mother cat turned her frightened eyes towards Emma and Casey.

"Look at that little brown one. It's so cute," Casey smiled.

"She's my favourite," said Emma. "I've called her Tiny. She's the only female, and the weakest kitten in the litter."

Emma felt sad as she stared down at her.

"Where did they come from?" Casey enquired. He looked puzzled as he moved closer to look at the young mother cat.

"They were in an alleyway, inside a cardboard box," Emma replied.

"I'm *sure* I've seen the mother cat before," said Casey. "I think she belongs to a man and his wife who live at the end of my road. They're not very nice. They own two vicious dogs. Once, when I was delivering newspapers, they jumped up at me. I was really frightened. The lady came out and shouted at me – told me to push off."

"Well, if they *do* own the little mother cat, I'm not surprised she had her kittens in an alleyway," said Emma, feeling angry. "It was probably a lot safer there."

Casey stood staring down at the mother and kittens. They had all dozed off to sleep.

"Let's leave them to sleep peacefully," said Emma.

Casey nodded, but as they walked towards the door the peace in the room was suddenly shattered.

"EMMA!" called Sue from the waiting room, her voice rising above a series of loud screeches. Immediately the mother cat's eyes opened wide again and her body stiffened.

"I'll be back, Casey," said Emma, rushing from the room. "Watch over them for me – and *no* touching."

* * *

The waiting room was filled with loud squawking. Sue called to Emma above the noise.

"Your dad's gone out on an emergency call, and Jack's taken over." She shuffled papers around her desk, searching for a pen to take details of a lady on the other end of the telephone.

Emma reached for the ballpoint Sue had absentmindedly stuck behind her ear.

"Thanks," Sue shouted above the din. "*Please*, help me by showing that irritable bird into the surgery. The racket he's making is upsetting some of the other animals – not to mention giving me a headache."

"Of course, but then I must go back to the kittens. I've left Casey with them," Emma replied. She winced as she stared in disbelief at the creature making all the noise. Taking the patient's details card out of the tray, she called:

"CAPTAIN!"

In reply came a wolf-whistle followed by a croaky voice.

"*Where's my grub? Where's my grub? Feed*

me! Feed me!" squawked the bird from a large metal cage. Only a few feathers, on top of its head, remained to identify it as the parrot described on the card and not some alien life form.

Cats mewed and dogs barked their annoyance in a dreadful chorus. The parrot's owner, a small, shy-looking man, stood up. He looked embarrassed.

"Sorry about the noise, but he gets a bit rowdy when he's feeling nervous," he said.

"*Nervous*," thought Emma. "I'd hate to hear him when he's feeling confident."

A door to one of the surgeries opened and Emma's tall, red-haired brother Jack strode into the waiting room.

"So – *this* is the creature that's been making so much noise." Jack smiled and beckoned to Emma to bring the bird and its owner into the surgery.

"No offence, but I'm afraid Captain is very particular about who he sees," stated his owner, while the bird nibbled affectionately on the man's ear. "He's usually treated by Mr Hodges – he gets on with him."

"Well I'm sorry, but my dad has been called out on an emergency. I'm Mr Hodges *junior*," he announced with confidence. "No need to worry, I've had quite a lot of experience with birds. I'm sure Captain and I will get along just fine."

Jack stared at Captain and thought he had seen healthier-looking frozen chickens in the supermarket.

Captain's owner still looked apprehensive. "You see, if he's nervous with new people, he tends to get a bit overexcited and has been known to peck." He thought for a moment before adding: "In fact he can be downright vicious when he's in the mood."

Jack remained confident. "During my long training as a vet I've been kicked by an angry horse, had a bull almost crush me against a wall, and a cat cling from the end of my nose. However, I'm proud to say, that never has a bird, of any description, pecked me. Welcome aboard, Captain! I think you've already sensed I'm in charge of *this* ship."

Stepping closer to look at Captain, Jack continued. "Seems to me as though this parrot is suffering from stress. All he probably needs is a course of vitamins and some gentle reassurance."

Captain thrust his head towards Jack and eyed him suspiciously from dark, beady eyes surrounded by scaly, grey flesh. Full of apprehension, his owner followed Jack into the surgery.

"Thank you, Em, but I don't think I'll be needing your help," said Jack. "I'll just get Captain out of his cage and spend a few moments gaining his confidence."

Returning to Sue, Emma said: "I'll be back in a minute. I need to check on Casey and the kittens."

Emma had barely made it out of the waiting room when a shriek, louder than anything Captain had produced, made everyone jump. The surgery door flew open and Jack burst into the waiting room.

"*MY FINGER!*" he howled, thrusting his hand in front of Sue.

"Look at the gash across the top of my finger. That beast attacked me. It's not a *parrot*! It's some kind of *fiend*!"

Captain's owner stood framed in the doorway, trying to calm the irate, squawking bird. He had managed to get him back in his cage. But Captain sat with his head almost squeezed through the bars, as though desperate to launch another attack upon Jack.

"I *said* he was a bit nervous," stressed his owner.

Captain emitted a low rumbling sound, like a broody hen, and stared menacingly at Jack through narrowed eyes.

Sue reached for the first-aid box, and Emma tried to calm the restless animals in the waiting room. A woman fought to gain control of her large dog, but it strained so hard at its leash that it broke free. In several leaps the dog was across the room, making a frenzied dash towards the rooms off the surgery.

Casey looked up, startled by the sudden arrival of the huge dog in the kittens' room. The pen housing them was open wide as Casey struggled with some soggy bedding near the kittens.

In a moment, the dog bounded over to the pen and thrust his head and one big paw through the opening. Terrified, the mother cat leapt up. In an attempt to defend her kittens, she hissed and spat at him. The huge dog lunged out with his paw. Taking a swipe at her, but missing, his fat paw landed in the middle of the fluffy bundle of sleeping kittens.

"*OH NO!*" shrieked Emma, arriving on the scene with the dog's owner, just in time to see the attack. With claws unsheathed, the dog lashed out again and delivered another blow. It scattered the kittens around the pen like soft, furry skittles.

"*TIMBER – LEAVE!*" shrieked his owner. "*LEAVE!*"

Reluctantly, the huge dog backed slowly away from the pen.

"I've got him!" shouted his owner, gripping Timber's collar.

Emma rushed to close the pen, but it was too late to prevent the shaken mother cat from dashing out.

Terrified of a further attack from the dog,

the little cat ran crazily around the room, before bolting out of the door.

"I'll catch her!" yelled Casey, dashing after her.

The frightened creature ran from room to room until, finding the back door to the garden ajar, she made her escape.

"What's going on?" called Jamie. He was carrying an armful of supplies in from the outhouse as the cat shot past him with Casey in pursuit.

"Quick! Stop her," shouted Casey, unable to prevent the cat scampering up a tree, and leaping on to the outhouse roof. With ears back and a wild look in her eyes, she sat trembling.

"You poor little things," said Emma, as she checked each kitten for injuries. "Midnight, Shadow and Socks – you seem to be all right. It's a miracle that dog didn't cause you any serious harm, apart from frightening your mum away. Don't worry, we'll get her back."

Emma carefully lifted up Tiny. "Now for you, my precious." Suddenly, she noticed a trickle of blood oozing from a gash that ran the length of Tiny's tail. "Oh no! You've been hurt. That's the last thing you need."

"Looks nasty!" announced Jack, entering the room and immediately seeing the gash in Tiny's tail. He held up his injured finger, covered in a bandage, for Emma to see. "My finger's swollen and throbbing like mad, thanks to that featherless bird of prey, but perhaps I can be of some help."

Emma placed Tiny on the work surface. "During all the commotion in the waiting room, a dog broke loose and lashed out at the kittens. He caught Tiny's tail with his paw. Fortunately the other kittens weren't hurt, but the mother cat has run off."

Jack shook his head. "She's taken quite a blow," he said, moving in for a closer look. "This weak little thing could do without having to fight off infection. I'm going to clean the tail with an antiseptic wash, dress it and give her an injection of antibiotics."

"Perhaps I'd better clean and dress it, if your finger is bandaged," offered Emma.

"Good idea, but first hold her still while I give her an injection."

Emma cradled the little, sleepy kitten in her hands as Jack prepared the syringe. "Gently does it," he whispered to himself. He inserted the needle into the loose, soft skin at the back of Tiny's neck. "There – let's hope that helps." Jack turned his attention to Tiny's injury, watching as Emma attended to it.

Her fingers worked skilfully as she cleaned the tail with a mild antiseptic solution, then wound a minute bandage around the gash to keep it clean. When she had finished, she placed Tiny next to her brothers, where the kitten soon drifted off to sleep.

"I'm going to see if Jamie and Casey had any luck in getting the kittens' mother back," said Emma.

She walked out into the garden, immediately alarmed by the sight of Jamie balancing precariously on the outhouse roof. He stood on tiptoe, with both feet in the old guttering. Just out of arm's reach the little mother cat sat poised, ready to dash off at the slightest disturbance.

"Come on, puss!" he coaxed. "Just move a

bit nearer to me and I can take you safely back to your kittens."

Jamie stretched one arm a little further towards her, and raised one leg to push his body higher up the roof. Several tiles shifted beneath his feet and fell with a clatter to the ground, causing him to lose his balance. He dug his fingers into the roof to stop himself from slipping.

"*Jamie!*" gasped Emma, clamping her hand across her mouth.

Frightened by the sudden shriek and noise of the falling tiles, the mother cat fled along the roof before jumping on to the garden wall. With ears back, appearing more terrified than ever, she took one fleeting look behind her. Then she was off, running along the wall that joined the back of the gardens to one another.

"Hang on, Jamie! I'll fetch a ladder. Just hang *on*!" cried Emma. She grabbed Casey to help her drag an old ladder from the garden shed.

"I can't hold on much longer," Jamie shouted, slipping further down the roof.

Emma and Casey fought to manoeuvre the wobbling old ladder as near to Jamie's feet as possible.

"Left foot back and down!" Emma yelled, watching Jamie's foot waving around as it groped for a foothold on the ladder.

"Got it!" he called.

"Now the right foot!"

Another tile fell to the ground, just missing Casey. Jamie followed Emma's directions by bringing his other foot on to the rung. Very slowly he descended the ladder.

"Sorry, but it looks as though I've scared her off," he said, touching ground. He brushed his trousers and checked his limbs for injuries. "Bruised shins and grazed elbows – could have been much worse."

"Don't apologize. It's my fault we've lost her. I shouldn't have screamed out," Emma volunteered.

"No," insisted Casey. "If *I* hadn't opened the kittens' pen, this would never have happened. I thought I was helping by mopping up some water the mother spilled when she got up to stretch."

"Look, it's no one's fault in particular," Jamie suggested. "But we can't stand here wasting valuable time; we should be trying to get the mother cat back. She's got a good start on us."

"You're right," agreed Emma. "The kittens need her – especially Tiny."

Crouching low on a wall overlooking a long, overgrown garden, the kittens' mother paused. She felt confused: drawn to her kittens, but too terrified by the dog to return.

Weak, hungry and in need of somewhere to hide and rest, she looked nervously about her. An old shed, half-buried in the overgrown garden, lay below the wall. One leap took her into the long grass close to it. The shed door was slightly open; the little cat peered inside. At the far end she saw a pile of old sacks. She crept warily inside, becoming suddenly aware of how dark it had grown. The sacks felt comfortable beneath her as she flopped down and fell asleep.

A gentle breeze turned into a gust of wind. It blew against the old shed door that creaked, as it slammed shut with a crash, waking and startling the little cat. Her eyes flashed as she rushed at the door, scratching at it trying to force it open, but it was shut tight – and she was trapped inside.

Chapter 4

Emma, Jamie and Casey searched the streets and the alleyway where the mother cat and her kittens had been found. They knocked at all the houses close to the clinic, asking the residents to check their gardens for the small black cat.

"There's no point knocking on *that* door," said Casey, as Emma sprang up the path of a very old house with dusty windows and torn net curtains. "It's been empty for ages."

"Looks spooky," said Emma, peering through the letterbox into gloomy rooms. "Only ghosts in there, I reckon, and ones that don't like cutting the grass, by the look of it. I can see right through the kitchen to the garden. It's like a jungle with an old shed at the end among the weeds. This place gives me the shivers. Let's go."

"Almost an hour of knocking on doors and no one has seen as much as a whisker of the kittens' mother. It's as though she's just vanished." Emma sighed, feeling tired. "Let's try the house where you thought the cat used to live, Casey."

Casey led Jamie and Emma through a broken wooden gate, past piles of old car tyres and some rotting rabbit hutches. Next to them, the remnants of an old motorbike rusted into the ground.

Emma stepped forward and rang the doorbell. It made an unpleasant buzzing sound that set off loud barks inside the house. After waiting two minutes without a response, she tried again. This time there was movement in the hallway. Through grimy, frosted glass panes in the door, she could see a dark silhouette stomping towards her.

"Shut up, Rebel! Quiet, Fury!" a husky voice bellowed.

Feeling nervous, Emma took a deep breath as the door was opened forcefully by a bulky woman who seemed to fill the doorway. An odour drifted out that made Emma want to recoil from the doorstep. A mixture of musty furnishings, cooked cabbage and the meaty smell of dogs, filled her nostrils. One of the woman's hands was grasped so tightly around the collar of a large black-and-tan dog, that the knuckles showed white under the strain. Snarling, and desperate to push past its owner, another big dog glowered at Emma and showed its teeth.

"If you're selling anything then I don't want it. And I don't give to charities!" announced the woman, starting to push the door shut.

"We're not trying to sell anything," Emma replied, keeping one eye on the dogs. She thought they looked as though they were about to break free at any moment. "We're looking for a young mother cat. My friend here seems to think you own one. Do you have a cat that's recently gone missing?"

"What's it got to do with you?" the woman snapped suspiciously.

"The veterinary clinic, where I live, has been caring for her and her kittens since we found them in an alleyway," Emma answered. "Unfortunately, the mother was startled; she's run off. That's why we are trying to find her – the kittens need her."

"Kittens, did you say?" answered the woman with a sly look on her face. She opened the door a little wider. "Since you ask, I do have a cat – sneaked off a week ago. But if she's had her kittens, then I reckon they belong to me, too."

Emma looked at the dogs, showing the whites of their eyes and dribbling from gaping mouths, full of sharp yellow teeth.

"I'm afraid I need to ask you to describe the cat to convince us we're talking about the same animal," she ventured.

"For your information, my cat is very small and black all over. Sly little thing – always creeping about, hiding in the house or staying out for days," hissed the woman.

Emma looked at the others, who nodded

their heads in agreement that the woman had given an accurate description of the kittens' mother.

"See," announced Casey. "I told you I thought she came from here."

"So, she's had her kittens, has she? *Good*. Then it's my right to demand my cat and my kittens back! I've got buyers lined up for them."

Emma felt her face flush and her temper rising. She looked at the huge, angry dogs and imagined the mother cat, Tiny and the other kittens trying to survive in such a threatening environment.

"Hasn't it ever entered your mind that the little cat was probably so afraid of those two vicious dogs, that she ran away to protect herself and the kittens she was expecting?"

"Look, if you've got my cat and her kittens," shouted the woman, thrusting her greasy face close to Emma, "then I want them back!"

"I'm sure there's no way my father would discharge the mother and her kittens into your care, especially with those dogs around.

All you seem concerned about is selling the kittens. If you want to take the matter further, then perhaps you'd like to come to the clinic and speak to my father, the vet."

Emma's bright eyes flashed and the woman glared back at her.

"Oh, keep the wretched things! *Cats* – they're nothing but a lot of bother."

Emma was about to speak when the dogs were dragged back by their collars and the door slammed abruptly in her face.

"Well," she sighed. "She seems to prove the theory that some owners resemble their dogs! I only hope the little mother cat doesn't turn up at this awful place ever again."

Emma walked back to the clinic with Jamie and Casey, to find there had been no sign of the mother cat. Eager to see if Tiny was all right, she peered into the pen and saw all the kittens were mewing hungrily, except the little tortoiseshell with the bandaged tail.

"Now we know why that poor young mother cat left such a hostile home to have her kittens," observed Mr Hodges, when Emma told him about the cat's owner. "But it still doesn't help our immediate situation. The kittens are in need of feeding. At their age they need feeding every two to four hours. So, without their mum around, you and I, Emma, are going to have to stand in for her. We are going to feed them on a milk substitute I've mixed."

He held up what looked to Emma like a doll's feeding bottle with a tiny teat on the end. "And this is what we'll use to feed them," he said.

Emma smiled. "I hope they take to it," she said. "And – I hope I'm capable of feeding the kittens. I've never done it before."

Emma said goodbye to Jamie and Casey, who left clutching Hercules' box safely under his arm.

"I'll keep a look out for the mother cat and tell my friends to watch out for her, too," called Casey as he left.

"And I'll take Buster for an extra long walk later on. That dog could spot a cat a mile away," added Jamie.

"Right Emma," said Mr Hodges, lifting Socks from the pen. "Let's see if we can get these ferocious beasts to take some milk."

He handed her a little feeding bottle filled with the milk substitute.

"You take Socks, and I'll start with Midnight."

Emma took the soft, furry bundle, still with his eyes tightly closed. He made little squirming movements in her hands.

"Now, Emma, just gently introduce the tip of the teat to the side of the kitten's mouth – like this," said her father. Emma watched as Midnight latched on to it and began to suck vigorously.

Emma attempted the same manoeuvre with Socks.

"Oh dear! He's turning his head away. He doesn't seem to want any."

"Don't worry. Be patient and try again," urged the vet.

With nervous hands, she persevered, but Socks's mouth remained shut. The milk dribbled from the bottle and ran over his soft coat on to Emma's hand.

"Oh, Dad," she sighed, "I'm doing it all wrong. Socks just doesn't want to know."

"Try to stay calm, Emma. He's probably picking up on how tense you're feeling. Just wait a bit. He *must* be hungry by now. As soon as some of it trickles into his mouth, and he tastes it, he should get the flavour for more."

She tried again. A little at a time she moved the tip of the teat into Socks's minute, pink mouth. This time the little kitten took it and began to guzzle greedily.

"Hey, Dad! He's taking it."

Socks soon gulped down the entire contents of the feeder bottle.

"Shall I give him some more?" Emma asked, smiling at the milky droplets around the kitten's mouth.

"You could try – see if he wants another one," Mr Hodges suggested. "He'll let you know when he's had enough."

Emma put another feeder bottle, full of the liquid, into the corner of Socks's mouth. Immediately he sucked at it.

"You little *piglet*. You've got the hang of it

now," she laughed. "I can feel your tummy beginning to fill up like a balloon."

She put Socks back in the pen, when he had taken most of another bottle, and he settled immediately into a contented sleep.

"Midnight has had all he wants, too," said Mr Hodges, replacing the kitten and reaching for Shadow.

At first, Shadow behaved exactly as Socks had done by refusing to take the milk, but eventually he took a full feeder.

Emma lowered her hand into the pen and lifted out her favourite kitten.

"Poor Tiny. I must be careful not to touch your tail. You feel so light after Socks. Even Casey's hamster must weigh more than you."

"Take it very slowly," Mr Hodges advised. "I'll be surprised if she takes much at all."

Emma looked at the little bundle of fur with the minute bandage on her injured tail. She felt pity for the little creature. Holding her gently, to avoid the kitten's tail, she put the tip of the teat in the side of her mouth. Tiny showed no interest. A few drops trickled down her chin. Emma waited then tried again, but the same thing happened.

"She's just not interested, Dad, and she feels sort of floppy."

· Mr Hodges put Shadow back in the pen next to Socks and Midnight, now both fast asleep. "Let me try," he said, taking Tiny from Emma's hands.

He placed the very tip of the teat in the corner of Tiny's mouth. For a moment it stayed in the kitten's mouth, but she didn't suck. Mr Hodges tried again. A slow smile spread across his face as Tiny began to draw slowly at the milky substance.

"Brilliant," Emma exclaimed. "Well done, Tiny."

"She's had enough by the look of it," said Mr Hodges. "Half a feeder full. That's a lot better than I imagined," he said, handing Tiny to Emma, while he reached for a tissue to wipe Tiny's mouth.

Emma stroked the kitten's soft head with her forefinger.

"Clever Tiny. You're a good girl. I wish I could stay here and cuddle you all day, but I don't think Dad would approve. Now snuggle up to your brothers and keep warm."

She knelt and placed Tiny close to the other contented kittens.

"I hope we *can* get the mother cat back," sighed Mr Hodges. "Of course it's not impossible to raise such young kittens without her, but it would certainly help to have her back and feeding them. I felt sure she would be concerned and have put in an appearance by now."

A soft sneeze came from the pen.

"It's Tiny," said Emma, frowning. "She's brought up her feed."

Mr Hodges reached inside the pen to clean Tiny and check that she hadn't got any of the feed in her nostrils.

"She will be all right, won't she, Dad?"

"I'll be honest, Emma, I really can't say. She's weak and *very* young – it could go either way at this stage. I'm going to put them all under infrared lights, and place a sheepskin blanket beneath them. It's so important to keep them warm."

When the kittens were settled, Emma

plodded reluctantly up the stairs to read. But Tiny, with her injured tail and frail little body, kept popping into her mind and she found it difficult to concentrate.

Chapter 5

Early Sunday morning the mother cat woke up in the dark shed. She felt feeble when she stood up and stretched her thin legs. Hungry and thirsty, she sniffed the air and looked around. Scrambling from one pile of discarded junk to another, she made it to a shelf and picked her way along it, sniffing and investigating the odd assortment of objects. But she found nothing edible among the dusty old jars, half-full of murky liquids, and rusty tins of paint.

Jumping to the floor, she crept cautiously to the door where a narrow beam of light fought its way in through a crack. Nose pressed to it, she breathed in the chilly morning air. Carefully she pushed one little black paw beneath the door and touched the grass on the other side, longing to get out again. Her paw felt for gaps, but she found none big enough to wriggle through. Disheartened, she made her way back to the sacks and lay staring up at clouds passing across the dirty window, high up in the shed.

"How are they today?" asked Emma, finding her father giving the kittens an early morning feed.

"Still pretty much the same as yesterday. Midnight, Shadow and Socks have been taking their feeds, but Tiny has been bringing hers up each time. Let's hope there's a sign of her mother today. Her presence would, at least, comfort Tiny."

Emma looked thoughtful. "I can't believe she would just desert them. I only hope that dog hasn't frightened her off for good. I'll carry on looking for her today. Jamie will probably help me. He's keen to keep checking in this area."

Emma arranged to meet Jamie by the

alleyway where they had found the kittens. They searched it again and called at more houses further afield, but still there was no sign of the mother cat. Once, their hopes were raised when Emma spotted a small black cat in the distance. It sat cleaning itself on a low wall, in front of a shop. She thought it looked a lot like the kittens' mother. As they crept closer to it, the cat turned to show white face markings and one white paw.

Emma and Jamie returned to the clinic at the end of another fruitless search. Immediately, Emma wanted to visit the kittens. To her dismay she discovered that Tiny was still bringing up her feeds.

"You'll have to face it, Emma," said her father, "Tiny is quite sickly. You must be brave if you want to make a good vet one day."

"I know, but just look at the poor little thing, lying there with her injured tail. She hasn't had a very good start in life – and even *that* may be a short one."

As another day drew to a close, the little mother cat got up off the sacks in the shed and wandered to the door. For the fourth time that day she mewed pitifully, desperate to be out of her cold, dark prison. Weak and hungry, she returned to the sacks, curled up and slept.

Chapter 6

"Has the mother cat come back?" asked Casey early Monday morning when Emma opened the front door and showed him into the waiting room.

"I'm afraid not. Jamie and I looked for her again, yesterday – but no luck. I bet you've come early so you can spend some time with Hercules before his operation."

"That's right," agreed Casey, sitting down with the hamster's box in his lap.

"I'm just going to put the kittens' feed out for Dad, and check that Tiny's bandage is still in place. Midnight, Shadow and Socks are feeding really well now. I wish I could say the same for Tiny."

As Emma busied herself preparing the feed, she looked at the kittens in the pen.

"All of them, except Tiny, seem to have grown even bigger over the weekend," she thought, as she heard the front door open and Sue arrive for work.

Taking one last opportunity to look at Tiny and her brothers before school, Emma knelt down at the side of the pen. She pressed her face so close to the wire that she could see the rise and fall of their little bodies as they breathed. Shadow, Socks and Midnight made stirring movements in their sleep, before they woke, but Tiny just lay still.

Emma felt her heart go out to the poor little kitten with the injured tail.

"Everything is so peaceful here. I wish I could stay and cuddle you, Tiny," she said. "The least I can do for you is find your mum, and I won't stop looking until I *do*."

The peace of the morning was suddenly shattered by Sue's raised voice.

"Oh no, Casey! That's a great start to the day – Hercules on the loose in the waiting room. We'll have to find him before any patients arrive. We can't have him popping his head up when there's a room full of people with their pets."

"Sorry – he just sort of slipped out of my hands – and *vanished*," Casey apologized, looking uncomfortable.

Emma rushed into the room in time to hear Casey's explanation. "'I'll help search for him, too," she said. "He can't have gone far."

Dropping to her knees, she began to look under all the chairs. Sue searched the area behind her desk, and Casey peered among the displays of cat and dog food.

As Emma scrambled about on the floor she was suddenly aware of a pair of shiny, brown shoes standing in front of her. Looking up, she found herself staring into her father's face.

"Let me guess," he said, smiling. "Could this possibly involve one golden hamster – owned by Casey?"

"He just slipped out of my hands, honest, Mr Hodges."

"Well, I'm sure he's still in here, somewhere. Sue and I will find him. I think it's best if you and Emma both head off to your schools."

"Yes, come on, Casey. My dad's right. I'll walk with you."

"I've fed the kittens and searched the room they're in, just in case Hercules had made his way in there. I hope he turns up soon; I'd planned to remove his lump later this morning," said Mr Hodges, walking into reception.

Sue shrugged her shoulders and frowned. "I'll keep my eyes open."

She patted Old Vic, gave him a doggy choc drop, then busied herself with the mound of paper work on her desk, occasionally looking up in the hope of seeing Hercules. Old Vic raised his head and whoofed at the sound of Jack thundering downstairs.

"Well, that definitely isn't the patter of tiny hamster paws I can hear," said Sue.

"Morning Sue," Jack announced, bounding into the surgery. "My finger has stopped throbbing at last, so I'm ready for action – but spare me from any bald parrots answering to the name of Captain."

Sue smiled, then noticed a sudden change of expression on Jack's face.

"SShh! DON'T MOVE!" he mouthed silently. He held one finger to his lips and pointed, with his bandaged one, to a pile of papers on Sue's desk. Her eyes opened wide, as the papers appeared to shuffle themselves around.

"It's Hercules – Casey's hamster," Sue whispered.

"Leave him to me," Jack replied.

"Be careful, Jack; he might bite."

Creeping forward on tiptoe, as though stalking a much larger beast, Jack advanced. Sue stared, watching the papers move again. As the hamster's tiny brown head popped up from beneath a pile of envelopes, Jack sprang. In one leap his long body seemed to sail through the air. Landing flat on Sue's desk, his hands closed around the small wriggling form. Beaming, he looked up into Sue's startled face and loosened his grip on the hamster. Its minute head emerged from between his fingers.

"There you go, little fellow," he said tenderly, stroking the creature with his bandaged finger. "You're safe and sound now."

"*Please* put him down, Jack, and get a cage for him. I don't like the way he's looking at you. I think he's unhappy you disturbed his walkabout."

"You wouldn't hurt *me*, would you, Hercules?" Jack smiled.

It wasn't until he was holding the creature up for a closer look, that it suddenly opened its mouth, exposing two long front teeth, both as sharp as needles. Before Jack had a chance to put Hercules down, the hamster sank the teeth deep into Jack's bandaged finger.

"*ARGHH!*" he hollered, so loud that Sue staggered backwards and Old Vic crept down from his chair and hid under the desk. Jack's shouts filled the air as Hercules continued to stay clamped to the wounded finger.

"Get this monster *off* me!" he bellowed.

Sue leaned over the desk and attempted to

work out the best way to remove Hercules, afraid he would turn on her if disturbed.

Mr Hodges burst into the waiting room and immediately assessed the situation. Grabbing Hercules gently but firmly from behind, he carefully prised the creature's jaws from Jack's finger.

"Your surprise move – that's what did it, Jack. You should have known better. The creature felt threatened, and defended itself," said Mr Hodges as he replaced Hercules in his box. "More caution next time," he said, taking the hamster away to remove its lump.

As Sue unwound the bandage around Jack's finger, he squealed as it tugged on the fresh wound.

"Just hold on a moment," she said when the doorbell rang.

"Hurry back!" Jack sighed, slumping into Sue's chair and closing his eyes. "I think I'm going to faint."

"This is Miss Roberts," announced Sue, returning with a young woman and her puppy. "Your dad asked her to bring in

Chips, her Labrador pup, for his vaccination. I was just explaining to her how you'd been wounded."

Jack sat up slowly. With an agonized look playing about his features, he turned to face the young woman. When he saw how pretty she was, he immediately put on a brave face.

"I'm a nurse," she said in a soft voice. "That looks a nasty wound. Would you like me to take a look?"

Jack sat up straight, and adopted a confident expression. He lowered his voice.

"*This?*" he gestured, making light of his throbbing finger. "It's nothing – really. Us vets are used to this sort of thing, you know – all in a day's work." He beamed, trying to mask the intense pain he was feeling.

Sue put her hand to her face to stifle a giggle.

"All the same, I think it would be a good idea if you let me look at it," persisted Miss Roberts. Chips sidled up to Jack and tugged playfully at his trouser leg. "He really likes you."

Jack sat back and smiled at the young nurse

as she bathed his finger in warm water and disinfectant.

"I hope you're not going to faint now, Jack," said Sue, with an impish smile on her face.

"Faint – *me*? How ridiculous!" he said, hoping Sue wouldn't make any further reference to his earlier outburst.

"*Please* tell me Tiny has taken some milk, or the kittens' mother has returned, Dad." Emma dropped her school bag on the kitchen floor.

"Sorry, Em. I wish I could, but Tiny is still bringing up any milk I manage to get down her, and there certainly hasn't been any sign of her mother."

"How about Tiny's tail?"

"Well, it doesn't look too bad, apart from swelling around the gash. But that should soon go down," Mr Hodges replied.

Emma still felt sad.

"I've operated successfully on Hercules, though," added Mr Hodges, trying to cheer her up. "Now there's one good bit of news for you – or at least for Casey."

"Oh great! Thank goodness you found him. Casey will be calling in on his way home from school. He was so worried when Hercules disappeared."

"I told you we'd find him. Actually, it was Jack who found him – about the same time as Hercules found Jack's injured finger."

Mr Hodges winced at the thought of the hamster's attack.

"Ouch! You mean Jack has been bitten *again* – and on the same finger? He must be in agony."

Mr Hodges' expression turned to a smile when he recalled the outcome of the incident. "Quite the opposite. In a strange way, I think, Jack is grateful to Hercules for bringing him into contact with a rather lovely young nurse. She dressed his wound."

Emma screwed her face up, puzzled by her father's remark. Before she had a chance to press him on it, Jack wandered into the room with a faraway expression on his face and sat down at the kitchen table.

"Don't you think Kirsty is a *beautiful* name?" he sighed, gazing out of the window.

"Nurse *Kirsty* Roberts," he added and sighed again contentedly.

"Ugh! It looks as though this animal has a hopeless case of lovesickness," said Emma. "I'm off to see the kittens."

Emma opened the door to the kittens' room, delighted to see Midnight, Shadow and Socks making little movements around their pen. Tiny was awake but lying still, showing no interest in the activity of her brothers.

"Come on, Tiny," cooed Emma, putting her little finger through the wire to stroke the kitten's head. "*Please* get stronger for me. I know your mum's not here to care for you and feed you her special milk, but we all want you to survive. Only you can do it."

She could feel a lump in her throat and wanted to cry at the sight of the skinny little kitten.

Emma sat looking at Tiny for ages and thought hard about where the kitten's mother could have gone. She thought it was strange that no one had even seen her.

"Are you all right down there?" asked

Jamie from the other side of the pen. "You're so locked into your thoughts, you didn't even hear me come into the room."

"Oh, hi, Jamie. You're right, I was thinking about the kittens' mother. She just seems to have vanished, and Tiny is getting weaker. I *know* she would stand a better chance if she had her mother back."

"When I cleaned the pen, earlier today, I was amazed by how light she felt compared to her brothers. If you want to go searching for her mother when I finish work, I'll join you. Perhaps we should put up notices: 'Small black cat – gone missing.' It might help."

"It's worth a try," said Emma, as Sue appeared around the door.

"Casey is in the waiting room. He's come to pick up Hercules, but he says he needs to tell you something important, Emma."

Emma followed Sue out to find Casey, beaming contentedly as he hugged the box containing Hercules close to his chest.

"Hello, Casey. I'm pleased Dad has removed Hercules' lump. Sue said there was something you had to tell me."

"When I was coming back from school, with my mates," said Casey excitedly, "we scrambled through a gap at the back of the houses along your road. It's a sort of short cut we've made. At the end of one garden, we're sure we heard a cat crying. It was coming from behind a really tall wall. We tried to climb it, but it was too high – even for *us*. You should have heard that cat – poor thing, sounded so sad. It might not be the kittens' mother, but I still reckon we should take a look."

Emma's eyes lit up. "What are we waiting for? Let's *go*!"

Chapter 7

Inside the dark old shed at the end of the deserted garden, the kittens' mother lay exhausted. She staggered around the shed every few hours to keep her limbs from stiffening, but had little energy left. From time to time she cried out, but no one came in response to her pleas to be set free.

"This is where we heard the cat," said Casey. "See what I mean about the wall – it's so *high*. I can't hear anything now, though, can you?"

Both Emma and Jamie listened, then shook their heads, agreeing with him.

"If you're sure this is the place," said

Jamie, "then I'd better take a look over the other side. You're right about it being high."

Jamie frowned, staring up at the wall that loomed over them, casting a cool, dark shadow. Remembering his recent incident on the outhouse roof, he stood back and assessed the best way to scale it. He handed his jumper to Emma.

"I think I can see a way to get up there, providing I can wedge my toes into the gaps in the brickwork."

Cautiously, he felt for hand and foot holds in the crumbling old wall and, little by little, moved towards the top. Halfway up he rested for a break.

"If I'd used my head I could have brought a ladder," called Emma.

"That's not a bad idea, but I'm almost there now."

In a few more swift moves Jamie scaled the wall successfully, raising both hands in a gesture of triumph, as he hauled himself to a sitting position astride it. He looked down into the garden on the other side and scanned the wilderness. He thought it showed traces of having once been a beautiful place, but weeds and brambles had fought and won a battle against the rosebushes and other flowers.

"The garden looks neglected and the house seems empty. Judging by its position, I think it must be the deserted house along your road, Emma."

"If it is, that would make it an ideal place for a cat to hide out and probably catch plenty to eat. Can you see or hear anything up there?" she asked.

Jamie inclined his head to concentrate on listening, and studied the garden for any signs of animal life.

"Nothing," he eventually replied. "But if I've come this far, I might as well search around for a bit."

"Be careful," said Emma.

"Do you want to pull me up, so I can help you look?" Casey asked, eager to join in the search.

"Best not," Jamie smiled as he slowly disappeared over the wall and slid down the other side.

The last bit of Jamie's descent landed him in a thick bramble bush. He could feel the prickles tangle around his legs. He had to pull them from his trousers before he could move on. Selecting a stick from a long-neglected pile of garden rubbish, Jamie hacked away at the undergrowth. Pausing at the shed, he noticed the door was shut and moved on.

Jamie made his way through the garden, prising apart the tall weeds, and prodding among the trailing bindweed that wound its way round the garden like a spider's web. He eventually reached the back of the deserted house and peered through the windows, thick with dust, at empty rooms. Checking the windows for gaps, just in case the mother cat had squeezed in, he found them all closed and secure.

Jamie criss-crossed his way back along the garden towards the high wall.

"Sorry to disappoint you," he called out to Emma and Casey, still waiting patiently on the other side. "No sign of our cat – or any other cat for that matter."

As he swished his stick backwards and forwards through the tall weeds, it banged against the side of the old garden shed.

The little mother cat woke with a start at the sound. She felt confused – afraid of what might be out there, but desperate to escape. When the noise stopped, as Jamie moved on, she panicked and dragged herself to the door. Scratching at it with her claws, she meowed as much as her hoarse voice would allow, but her cries were faint.

Jamie had pulled himself halfway up the wall. He waited to catch his breath before reaching the top, and wiped his hot forehead with the back of his arm.

He took one last look at the garden, before pressing on towards the top. But as he dug his toecap into the brickwork, he thought he heard a faint mewing behind him.

Dropping down into the garden again, he crouched low in the undergrowth. The cat's cries had stopped. He trudged forward and immediately they began again. Listening intently, he traced the sound to the shed. He peered through the yellowing, dirty pane of glass and managed to see inside. Barely discernible in the poor light, he could see the weakened figure of the little mother cat, crying and clawing feebly at the shed door.

"I've found her!" he called out to Emma and Casey, creeping to the front and shaking the door handle. It had jammed shut, but with a couple of twists it gave way.

Jamie felt shocked to see how weak and dishevelled the poor little creature looked. He eased his way into the shed, but she didn't move.

Taking a bit of the sack she had slept on, he wrapped her up and carried her into the light. She didn't try to wriggle free, but just lay limply in his arms. To Jamie she felt as light as a feather. It was no effort for him to carry her, tucked into the front of his shirt, as he scaled the wall again.

"I've *got* her," he called again to the others. "She was shut in an old shed. I'm coming up now. She's very weak, but I think I can manage to get her over, just as long as nothing frightens her."

"*Brilliant*, Jamie!" Emma called back excitedly.

The little cat felt safe inside Jamie's shirt, even when she began to wobble about as he neared the top. Carefully swinging one leg over the wall, he sat for a few moments' rest before his descent.

"Is she still all right?" enquired Emma. "Perhaps I should go and get a cat basket."

"She's shivering a bit, probably with nerves, but I'll be down in a moment."

Jamie had only a few more steps to go before his feet touched the ground, when the incredibly loud buzz of a hedge-trimmer started up in a nearby garden. The noise burst upon the air, making Jamie, Emma and Casey jump.

"Steady, little one," Jamie said, trying to reassure the cat. Her small, frightened face peered out of his shirt.

"ZZZZZZZ." The high-pitched sound rose even higher.

Terrified, the cat dug her claws into Jamie's chest and pushed her way out of his shirt.

The sudden leap she made turned into a fall and she disappeared among the weeds in the garden.

"*Great!*" said Jamie. "We almost had her, if it hadn't been for that wretched noise starting up. I'm going down to try to find her again," he said, exhausted by the climbing. But before he made another move, he caught sight of her crawling her way over an adjoining garden fence and slinking down the other side.

"It's no good – she's gone! She's had another bad fright, so it would terrify her and drive her further away if we pursued the poor thing."

"I bet she's been in that shed all the time. At least she's free to return to the kittens, now," said Emma as Jamie's feet touched the ground.

Feeling frustrated after all their efforts, Emma, Jamie and Casey made their way back to the clinic in silence.

Chapter 8

"We were so near, Dad. Jamie had her in his shirt, then some awful-sounding hedge-trimmer thing started up and frightened her away!"

"Well, at least she's out in the open again. The best thing we can do is leave the window open in the kittens' room, in the hope she will return."

"How's Tiny, Dad?"

"No change, I'm afraid. I had a look at her tail. It's still tender and swollen. She's listless and not at all interested in feeding."

Emma frowned, saddened that their chance of getting the mother cat back had slipped away. Now the news about Tiny made her feel hope was running out.

Emma sat bolt upright in bed, waking from a dream. Locked inside an old shed, she had desperately tried to get out to the kittens, which were frantically scratching on the window in an attempt to reach her.

"Thank goodness it *was* only a dream," she sighed, running her hand through her hair, tangled from where she had tossed and turned in her sleep. She flopped back again on the pillow, staring up at the dark ceiling. Finding it impossible to return to sleep, and a little afraid to, in case the dream returned, she decided to go downstairs and check on the kittens.

Emma caught her breath as she opened the door to the kittens' room. On the other side of the window, she could make out the silhouette of a small cat. She kept low and watched it paw the window.

"*Please* be the kittens' mother," she whispered under her breath.

Emma looked at the kittens. They were

curled up together in a deep sleep. She stayed motionless as she watched the cat pull itself up to reach the open window-flap. As the moonlight was reflected on the cat's all-black coat, Emma felt sure it was the kittens' mother.

"Come on, little one," she said under her breath. "If you are the kittens' mum, they're really in need of you, especially Tiny."

Very cautiously, the little cat sat balanced on the window frame for a few moments, before dropping down on to a work surface. Emma could hardly contain her excitement.

"That's right – now over you go to your babies," she whispered.

For a few seconds the cat stood still and looked around, sniffing at the warm air inside the room. Nervously, she padded to the kittens' pen and extended a paw through the wire to touch them.

Emma felt her pulse racing as she tried to think what to do next.

"The window – if I can just creep across and shut it without scaring her."

She turned to shut the door behind her in

case the cat made a sudden dash. But as she pushed on it, the door resisted as someone pushed from the other side. Emma's heart pounded and she gasped. A hand appeared around the door, but when she saw the index finger was covered in a big, white bandage, she breathed a sigh of relief.

"Jack – you *twit*!" she whispered in his ear, as the rest of his body squeezed into the room.

"Sorry if I gave you a scare. I thought I heard someone creeping past my bedroom, and came to investigate. I had a feeling it was you checking on the kittens."

Emma put a finger to her mouth. "Sshh!" she whispered. "The kittens' mother has returned. She's with them by the cage, so no sudden noise. Do you think you could creep over and shut the window flap without distracting her? Then we'll have blocked off all her exits."

"No problem," replied Jack. "Leave it to me."

Emma watched the cat. From time to time she pricked up her ears, but soon returned to looking at her young ones. She sat as near as she could get to the fluffy bundles on the other side of the wire.

Like a ghost, Jack crept across the room to close the window. Kneeling on the work surface, and stretching up to close the flap, his shadow passed over the mother cat. Immediately, she stood on all fours and, with her back arched, stared at his outline against the window.

"She's seen you, Jack. Don't move!" Emma said, as calmly and as quietly as she could manage.

Jack remained still, frozen like a statue, but could feel himself beginning to topple over. He adjusted his position to prevent himself from falling. But in a moment of panic, the little mother cat jumped up and dashed around the room. Emma tried to catch her, but she was too fast. While Jack struggled to close the window, the cat suddenly leapt on his back. She ran along to his shoulders and on to his head, before squeezing through the flap. Unfortunately for Jack, the cat knocked the window catch as she disappeared into the night, and the full force of the window fell on his injured finger.

"*HELP! Em!*" he shrieked. "My *finger* – it's been crushed!"

Emma flicked on the light. Carefully, she lifted the window flap from Jack's finger, and he slumped to the floor like an old coat.

"You poor thing!" She could already see the base of his finger beginning to swell.

"Pecked, savaged and now *crushed*," Jack sighed. "I'll never be able to play my guitar again."

Later that morning, the entire Hodges family stood around Jack's bed.

"Elevate it, Jack," advised Mr Hodges. "You must keep it raised on the pillows to allow the swelling to go down."

"Look at it!" moaned Jack. "How can I work with a finger the size of a small marrow and the colour of beetroot?"

"You really should get a doctor to look at it," suggested Mr Hodges. "Three injuries to the same finger, in several days, would certainly warrant some stronger painkillers."

A smile broke across Mr Hodges' face. "I'd almost forgotten, Jack, Miss Roberts is bringing her puppy Chips in again this morning. She wants to discuss his diet with me. Perhaps I should send her up to see you?"

A transformation came over Jack's face. "*Kirsty*? She's coming here this morning? I must *wash*! I must *shave*!" he exclaimed, leaping from his bed and dashing to the bathroom to prepare.

Chapter 9

Emma looked in on the kittens. Her father had just finished feeding them.

"Did Tiny take any milk?" she enquired.

"I'm afraid not."

"Well I won't give up on her, Dad. I know her mother ran off again, but she *had* come back to see them. You should have seen her touch them through the wire. I just know she wants to care for them."

Mr Hodges stroked his chin and looked down at Tiny, who lay listlessly in the pen, while the others tumbled and fell over one another.

"I'll make sure things are kept as quiet as possible out here. The window is still open for their mother to get in. Now run along, or you'll be late for school."

Emma spent a miserable day at school, wishing the hours would pass quickly so that she could find out whether the mother cat had returned. The bell finally went for the end of the last lesson. She packed her bag and ran all the way home.

"Emma!" called Sue. "I've been longing for you to get back. The mother cat is back again. She crept in through the window. Jamie managed to shut it from the outside. He's opened the kittens' pen, hoping she will go inside so he can fasten it shut. You'll find him outside their room. He told me to let you know the minute you arrived."

"*Fantastic!*" shouted Emma, setting off the dogs in the waiting room.

She found Jamie kneeling at the door, peering through the keyhole.

"The mother is moving closer to the pen," he whispered. "Look, Emma – just look at that!"

Emma could hardly believe her eyes as she

squinted through the keyhole. "She's inside the pen – lying down – and the kittens are scrambling over one another to feed from her. This is wonderful!"

Very carefully Jamie eased open the door and, a little at a time, squeezed inside. The mother cat raised her head and looked at them.

"Stay *very* still," he warned Emma. "I'm going to make my way over to the pen."

Jamie lay flat on the floor and crept forward, commando-style, watching all the time for any reaction from the mother cat. When he reached the pen, he neatly swung the door shut and fastened it.

"They are all safely inside," he said. "You can come and have a look."

Emma stood above the pen staring down at the mother cat with her kittens. But when her gaze fell on Tiny, lying motionless amongst the bedding, she felt incredibly sad.

"Oh, *no*," she cried. "You don't think Tiny is dead, do you?"

Jamie peered closely at the kitten and shook his head. "I can't tell. Let's get Jack. Your dad's tied up with a difficult case."

Jack came to the kittens' room and immediately opened the pen door, carefully easing Tiny out. He placed her on the work surface and made a quick examination. "She's alive, Em, but very weak."

Emma could feel tears welling up in her eyes.

"I'm going to try something I once saw Dad attempt, but I really can't promise success. If I place Tiny next to her mother, she might just draw comfort from her and sense the need to feed."

"But she hasn't fed since we first brought them in from the alleyway."

"I can only try, Em. Never fail to be amazed by the way animals can surprise us – just when we think there's no hope, too."

Jack cradled Tiny in his hands and knelt down to squeeze her in among her brothers, taking care not to crush her tail.

"I think it's best if we just leave them," he suggested. "All we can do is hope she will feel the need to feed, now that her mum's back."

Emma, Jack and Jamie left the room.

"How long before we check on them?" Emma eagerly enquired.

"Let's give them a couple of hours," said Jack.

"I don't think I can wait that long," said Emma restlessly.

"Well I suggest that to take your mind off the situation, and aid your poor injured brother, you make me a cup of tea."

As Emma set about making tea in the little kitchen at the back of the clinic, her father appeared with an elderly lady. She held a handkerchief to her eyes and dabbed them as she wept quietly.

"Emma," said Mr Hodges. "I wonder if you would get Mrs Simpson a warm drink. She's being very brave."

Emma recognized the old lady. She also realized the implication of her father's words. Mrs Simpson's old cat, Bertie, had had to be put to sleep. Emma knew he had been seriously ill for months with no hope of recovery. The old lady found the decision hard. Bertie was her companion for sixteen years.

Emma put an arm around Mrs Simpson's shoulder. "Let's have some tea together, shall we?"

"That's very kind of you, dear," replied Mrs Simpson. "I knew I would have to face life without Bertie one day. I'm going to miss that old rascal," she said, trying to smile.

Emma sat for an hour while the old lady told her all about the good times she had spent with Bertie. Since she had taken him in as a stray, he had always slept at the end of her bed and sat on his own special chair next to her at breakfast.

"Perhaps, in time, you'll have another cat," suggested Emma.

"Oh, I don't think so, dear. There could never be another cat quite like Bertie."

"Well, should you change your mind, we have a mother cat and her four kittens in a room out the back. They will need homes in several weeks' time. The mother cat ran away from a very unpleasant owner. She had her kittens in an alleyway. If you'd like to see them, one day, I'd be pleased to show you."

Mrs Simpson looked thoughtful, and Emma's face fell when she remembered Tiny.

"I'm afraid one of them is very weak."

"I'm sorry to hear that, dear. I do hope the poor kitten improves."

Mrs Simpson's daughter came to pick her mother up. She thanked Emma for caring for her, and showed an interest in taking one, or possibly two, of the kittens when the time came. As soon as they had gone, Emma found Jack and pleaded for him to look at Tiny.

Jack agreed. Emma could see the mother cat and kittens dozing, but Tiny lying just where Jack had placed her.

"Come on, Emma," he said, trying to comfort her. "We'll keep them together overnight. Just keep hoping."

Emma cried herself to sleep that night. When she woke early the next morning, she crept downstairs and let herself into the kittens' room. Rubbing her eyes, she looked down into the pen. It was just as she had suspected. Three kittens eagerly sucked milk from their mother – and one lay apart from the rest.

As she turned to look for Jack or her father, to tell them that nothing had changed, she suddenly realized something was out of place in the pen. She looked at the kittens again.

The little kitten lying apart from the others, who were feeding greedily, was Shadow. He rolled over to expose a full and contented belly. Emma stared at the other kittens feeding – the smallest lay between her brothers.

"*TINY!*" she squealed, clamping a hand across her mouth. "You're *feeding!*"

Chapter 10

"Do you realize what time of the morning this is?" yawned Jack. "It's half past five! You had better have a good reason for disturbing my beauty sleep."

"*Tiny!*" said Emma excitedly. "She's *feeding*!"

"That's great!" said Jack, rubbing his eyes. "So my idea of putting her close to her mother worked after all. Let's just hope she keeps it up. Don't let anyone disturb them; it's important they continue to bond."

Emma could hardly wait for the rest of the family to get up. Her father was the next person she told when he appeared in the kitchen.

"Now this *is* a breakthrough," he said, dashing off to see for himself.

The moment Jamie came through the door, Emma pounced on him with her good news.

"Guess what?" she said, beaming.

"No need to guess," he smiled. "There's only one thing that could possibly make you so happy: Tiny is feeding?"

"Got it in one! I'm so pleased. It was Jack's suggestion to put her close to her mother – and it worked. I just *know* she will pull through."

"Look, Dad," Emma whispered when she joined her father in the kittens' room. "Tiny has curled up with the other kittens. She must have had her fill of milk."

"And she doesn't appear to have brought any up," Mr Hodges smiled. "I'll add vitamin drops to the mother's food again. She needs to build up her strength after her ordeal in that shed. Something else has happened, too. Look carefully at the kittens' faces."

Emma peered at the little furry faces. "Their eyes – they're sort of half open!"

"That's right," smiled the vet. "They open a little at a time and will be blue for a while."

To their surprise the mother cat stared up at Emma and her father and blinked.

"You're safe with us here," cooed Emma. "No need to run any more. I promise there won't be any big dogs to scare you away."

The cat began to lick Tiny's face gently, and a soft, gentle purring came from the mother and kitten. Emma felt so happy she wanted to purr herself.

As the days passed, Emma could see definite signs of improvement in Tiny. Occasionally she brought up her feed, but Mr Hodges seemed sure it was no longer anything to worry about. He removed the bandage around her tail. The gash had begun to heal, leaving a pink narrow line where the fur refused to grow. But it was free from infection. All the kittens had their eyes fully open and were developing lovely, fluffy coats. The mother cat started to look healthier as she took more of the fresh, nourishing food put down for her.

Another Saturday morning arrived and, as usual, Emma couldn't wait to get down to her weekly job helping out in the clinic. Before the patients and their owners arrived, her father made his daily check on the mother and kittens.

Taking great care not to frighten the mother cat, Emma extracted Tiny from the huddle of little bodies clustered around her.

"Come on Socks, you great big boy, move over; you're almost squashing Tiny. As for you two, Midnight and Shadow, we'll need to get a bigger pen, if you grow any more. I do believe you're putting on weight, too," she said to Tiny. "Your little tummy feels quite full."

The kitten's bright eyes stared up at her, and she began to purr.

Mr Hodges took the kitten and placed her on the work surface. He examined her eyes, the inside of her mouth and then turned his attention to her tail.

"Hmm," he said thoughtfully, stroking

Tiny. "You've given my daughter more than a few worries over the past weeks. She's grown *so* attached to you, I really think it would be a good idea if you stayed with her. What do you think, Em?"

"You mean I can *keep* Tiny?"

Mr Hodges nodded his approval, and Emma picked up the little kitten and snuggled her close, breathing in the warm smell of her fur.

"You've got two visitors waiting for you," said Sue as Emma glanced down her father's list of patients for the morning.

Emma looked up and saw Mrs Simpson and her daughter sitting at the far end of the waiting room.

"I can see you are busy, dear," began Mrs Simpson, "but my daughter and I have thought a lot about that little family of kittens you are caring for. I would love to take one kitten, and my daughter two of them, if your father agrees. How does that sound to you?"

"Sounds wonderful to me. I'm sure my dad would agree, too."

"The kittens are in a room at the back of the surgery, if you would like to see them. Dad won't miss me for a few minutes."

"Oh! They are just *beautiful*!" exclaimed the old lady as she caught her first sight of the sleepy kittens.

"Adorable," added her daughter.

"The whole family has come along very well, after a shaky start. Just a few more weeks and, if all goes well, they should be able to leave their mother. They're just learning to lap and move on to solid food."

Mrs Simpson looked sad for a moment. "I always think it must be a shame when the family has to be split up. The little tortoiseshell seems very attached to her mother." The old lady paused, deep in thought for a moment. "How would you feel about me taking the mother as well as that beautiful kitten, when they're ready to leave?"

"In that case," added her daughter, "why don't I take *three* kittens. I've masses of room in my house and garden. And as I live next door to my mother, it would be so lovely for the whole family to stay so close to one another."

Emma's head spun. The shock of the ladies' offer swept over her like a sudden burst of rain. Overwhelmed by the mixture of feelings she was experiencing, she didn't know whether to laugh or cry.

"Tiny and her mother won't have to be parted," she thought. "And the other kittens will live next door. The whole family will grow up together." She steeled herself and took a deep breath before answering.

"I think that is a *very* generous offer. But are you sure they wouldn't be too much for you to take on?"

"Certainly not for me," answered Mrs Simpson's daughter. "I have always had cats. There are two old ones at home now. My mother and I have enormous gardens and we're around all day. I think it would be wonderful to have a young family living with us – keep *us* young, don't you think so, mother?"

Mrs Simpson smiled. "I'll manage just fine."

"I'll need to speak to my dad about your offer, of course. He will probably want them to stay here for a few more weeks."

Still dazed, Emma told the ladies the kittens' names.

"Socks, Midnight and Shadow," she said, pointing to each kitten in turn. "They are all males."

"And what is the name of my *favourite* – the little tortoiseshell?" enquired Mrs Simpson.

"I named her Tiny. She is the only female in the litter. She's the one who was very weak, but she's a lot better now."

"Hello Tiny," cooed Mrs Simpson. "I can see I would make a great fuss of *you*."

Emma felt strange. "It's not too late to tell her Tiny is mine," she thought.

"There you are, Emma!" announced Mr Hodges, appearing around the door. "The waiting room is beginning to fill up. I'd like some help, please."

"I have some good news, Dad. Mrs Simpson has kindly offered to take the mother cat and Tiny, and her daughter has offered to have Socks, Midnight and Shadow, if that's all right with you."

A frown swept across Mr Hodges' face and he looked straight at Emma. But something about the expression in her eyes stopped him from mentioning that Tiny was her kitten. In an instant, he knew why she had decided to give her up.

He gave Emma a warm smile and said: "I think that is a *very* kind offer."

Before Emma showed Mrs Simpson and her daughter out, Mr Hodges spoke to them to ensure they weren't taking on too much. He had to agree the mother and daughter had perfect homes for the little family to grow up in.

"It's not too late, you know, Em," he said as soon as they had gone. "You had your heart set on keeping Tiny. I'd let you keep the mother cat as well."

"No Dad, I've made up my mind. I would rather the family stayed together after all they've been through," she answered. "Besides, the mother would never really be comfortable with dogs always coming into the clinic, even if we kept her well out of the way."

Emma dabbed at the corner of her eyes with her overall.

"I had better go and show your first patients in," she said, excusing herself as more tears began to form in her eyes.

Chapter 11

"This basket has Socks, Midnight and Shadow." Jamie handed Emma a cat carrier. She placed it on one side of her in the back of the car owned by Mrs Simpson's daughter. "And in this one you'll find Tiny and her mother. Are you sure you can manage, or would you like me to come with you in case they start to play up?"

"I'll be fine, thanks," replied Emma, wriggling to make herself comfortable before the short journey to where Mrs Simpson and her daughter lived. "I don't think there's room for you anyway," she smiled.

"I'm here to help," piped up Mrs Simpson from the front passenger seat.

Emma waved goodbye to Jamie as the little car drove the mother cat and kittens away to their new homes. She recalled it had been almost two months since she had found the kittens in the alleyway. She felt sad they were leaving, but pleased they were to remain so close to one another.

Emma had tried hard to get used to the idea that Tiny would be leaving. She knew she would miss her dreadfully.

Mr Hodges had made a thorough check in the morning and pronounced the kittens to be in a healthy condition. He felt they should adapt well to their new owners.

Emma had carefully packed up all the kittens' toys, a blanket and the mother cat's vitamin drops.

She was pleased the cat and her kittens remained calm throughout the journey. She had anticipated that at least one of them would not like the ride. But apart from one of Socks's little white paws emerging from a gap in the side of the basket, there had been no movement from them at all.

*　*　*

"Here we are, dear," smiled Mrs Simpson as her daughter pulled up outside two adjoining houses, in a quiet tree-lined road, a few miles away from the clinic. Emma took the basket containing Tiny and her mother out of the car; Mrs Simpson's daughter carried the other.

"Why don't you go in with my mother, Emma, while I introduce Socks, Midnight and Shadow to their new home. My two old cats will be fast asleep. They're in for quite a surprise when they wake."

Emma agreed and followed Mrs Simpson down the path and into her house. It was large but cosy inside. Mrs Simpson showed her into the sitting room. Emma saw a soft shawl, with the name Bertie embroidered on it. It was lying inside a large cat basket Mrs Simpson had prepared for the mother cat and Tiny.

"I think it would be a good idea for us to sit down and open the basket. Tiny and her mother will come out when they're ready," said Mrs Simpson.

Emma agreed and unfastened the straps on

the cat basket before cautiously opening it. She peered inside and saw the mother cat and Tiny curled up together. The mother looked up at her and blinked, but Tiny remained asleep. Emma sank into a big, comfortable, old sofa and waited while Mrs Simpson made some tea. Suddenly the mother cat popped her head over the top of the basket and looked around the room. Emma could see her nostrils twitching as she breathed in all the strange smells of her new environment. When she seemed satisfied that there was no immediate threat, she jumped out and made an inspection tour of the room.

Gradually she worked her way around the room sniffing the furniture and carpets. When Mrs Simpson returned, the mother cat froze on the spot, then quickly fled back to the safety of her basket.

Mrs Simpson set down the tea things.

As they sat down to enjoy their cup of tea, the top of the mother cat's head appeared above the edge of the basket again.

"Look!" whispered Emma.

Emma and Mrs Simpson sat as still as

statues while the cat stared at both of them in turn, then disappeared back into the basket. Within seconds she was back again, but this time carrying Tiny in her mouth.

"How *marvellous*!" said Mrs Simpson as the cat carried Tiny away to a space beneath an old desk in the corner of the room.

"I think that must be a fairly good sign that she's moving in," said Emma, watching Tiny undergo a thorough washing from her mother.

Emma and Mrs Simpson spent the rest of the afternoon together, talking about the kittens and their mother. The old lady took Emma out into her big garden, ideal for cats to explore. It was full of bushes, and had two trees to climb. Mrs Simpson's daughter appeared at a gate connecting the two gardens.

"Hi! How are Tiny and her mother getting along?" she asked.

"Just fine, by the look of it," answered Emma. "How about Socks, Midnight and Shadow?"

Mrs Simpson's daughter laughed. "All of them were out of the basket and chasing one another around the kitchen floor within minutes of arriving. They have already met my two old cats. I don't think the poor creatures are going to get much peace with the kittens around. Come and see for yourself."

Emma went in to take a last look at Tiny and her mother. Mrs Simpson had put a blanket, which Emma had brought with her, under the desk. After pawing it around to make it comfortable, she settled down with Tiny to sleep. Emma knelt beside them and watched as their sides rose and fell with each breath, and they slept on into their first day at their new home.

"Well, Tiny," she whispered, "I never thought I would see this day quite so soon. You're growing into a beautiful cat with the help of your mother. Even your little tail has healed." She sighed as she stood up. "I'm really going to miss you, but I promise I'll visit from time to time."

* * *

Mrs Simpson's daughter took Emma into her kitchen. She laughed when she saw Socks, Midnight and Shadow, rolling and tumbling in and out of a big cardboard box filled with blankets. Socks had managed to work his way underneath the blankets and the other two were leaping on him whenever he moved.

"They certainly seem to have taken to their new home," said Emma.

"I'm sure they are having too much fun playing to have noticed," smiled Mrs Simpson's daughter.

Emma approached the entrance to the clinic early in the evening. She chose to walk back from Mrs Simpson's house to get a breath of fresh air before going home. She thought it would seem unbearable there without the kittens.

She was so lost in thoughts about Tiny, that, at first, she didn't notice the strange eerie sounds drifting downstairs as she entered the house.

"*Don't* go into the front room, Emma. Kirsty Roberts has paid Jack an unexpected visit," said Mrs Hodges, as Emma reached the top stair.

"So what is that unbelievably horrible sound coming from the room? Do you think she's causing him pain?" Emma put her hands to her ears as a series of high-pitched shrieks burst upon the air.

"No dear, quite the opposite. Jack is playing some wildlife recordings he made during his stay in some remote jungle a few years ago," said Mrs Hodges. "He spent time studying the calls of different creatures to help him with a project at veterinary college. Poor girl – she's been sitting through it for over an hour now."

"Well if he thinks he's going to attract her with *that* kind of stuff, he'd better think again," replied Emma as the noise came to an abrupt end.

Emma heard the front room door open and Jack's voice booming as he walked Kirsty downstairs. She could hear Chip, her puppy, scampering along the floor.

"So – I'll call for you tomorrow, at about seven o'clock?" Emma heard Jack say.

She laughed. "Apparently Nurse Roberts *has* been attracted by the calls of a colony of apes."

Emma sat through dinner listening to Jack speaking on the one subject on his mind: Kirsty Roberts. Emma was pleased to have a diversion. But her thoughts occasionally wandered to the room downstairs, now containing an empty pen, where Tiny, Socks, Midnight, Shadow and their mother had stayed. She knew she would have to face the room sooner or later.

The telephone rang just as Emma and her family had started to clear away the dinner things.

"Is everything all right?" Emma enquired, fearing something had happened to the kittens or their mother, when she heard Mrs Simpson's voice at the other end.

"Yes dear – everything is just *fine*. I rang you because as I was putting out food for the little mother cat, I realized I didn't know her name. Has she got one?" the old lady enquired.

Emma frowned as she considered the question and realized that the little cat had always been referred to as the kittens' mother.

"I have to confess, Mrs Simpson, that I'd only named the kittens."

"Well in that case, I was wondering whether you would mind if I called her Emma – after you?"

Chapter 12

Emma walked into the clinic after school the following week. Sue the receptionist sat behind her desk giving Old Vic his last choc-drop of the afternoon.

"I think that's so sweet – the kittens' mother named after you," Sue beamed.

"So do I!" said Emma, patting Old Vic's bony head. "I feel quite honoured."

"By the way Em, Jack is taking surgery. Your dad has gone out on a call. He wondered if you could help out by looking in on a new case, in the back room."

"No problem," said Emma. "What is it?" she asked, as she dumped her bags behind the reception desk.

"He's left a note on the door," said Sue with a mysterious smile on her face.

The note was pinned to the door. In her father's handwriting Emma read: "PLEASE TAKE PERMANENT CARE OF THIS ANIMAL."

As soon as she set eyes on the little tortoiseshell kitten in the pen, she realized that, although it wasn't Tiny, it would take her only a short time to become very attached to her, and love her just as much.

When Mr Hodges returned home that evening, he walked into the front room to see Emma sitting with the little kitten on her lap.

"I made a home visit a week ago and they had some kittens. I knew how brave you'd been in giving up Tiny – so I found this one a *suitable home*."

Emma held the fluffy bundle up close to her chin and nuzzled the kitten's fur. "All I have to do now," she said, "is think of a *suitable name*."

Read another story about Emma

The Dog with the Wounded Paw

Turn over for a taster!

Chapter 1

A tall fourteen-year-old girl, her shoulders weighed down by two heavy school bags, made her way home along a busy North London road. One bag was stuffed full with muddy sports kit, the other groaned under the weight of text books. The girl, Emma Hodges, was wondering which of her homework assignments she should tackle first that evening.

As it was Friday she would try to clear as much of her homework as possible so that she could leave the weekend free – for what she considered to be far more exciting work. Maths, Emma decided, would get first attention. Best to dispense with the one she liked least of all; the others wouldn't seem so bad after that. She hurried on. It would only take another five minutes to reach home.

As Emma passed the last of the railings marking the entrance to her local park, she saw a small group of boys aged from sixteen to eighteen ahead of her. She steeled herself, prepared to ignore any remarks they might throw her way; she'd encountered the group before. It was the biggest member of the group who first spotted her, as he proudly displayed to his friends a new, black leather motorcycle-jacket. Beautifully illustrated on the back in orange, brown and gold paint was a tiger leaping through brilliant green jungle ferns. Beneath the picture, brass studs spelt out the boy's self-appointed name: TIGER.

"Carry your books, Miss?" he asked in a mocking tone, as he leapt to block Emma's path. She ignored him, neatly side-stepping out of his way, to the amusement of the rest of his group. Persisting in his fun, the boy sank to his knees. As Emma passed he implored with affected coyness,

"Oh, *please*! I only want to help you."

Emma struggled to keep her eyes focused straight ahead and continued to walk on – best to ignore them, not say a word. But something suddenly happened which made it impossible for her to stay silent. One of the boys had just lit a cigarette and casually flicked the spent match to the ground. From among the cluster of denim-covered legs, a slim, tan mongrel with soft, silky ears and large, appealing brown eyes emerged yelping and frightened. Emma saw that the short, tatty lead attaching it to the railings was preventing it from moving very far.

"You ought to watch where you throw your matches," she cautioned the boy with the cigarette. "You could have burned that poor dog. As it is, you've scared him witless."

The lad laughed out loud. "Scared! Buster? He's scared of nothing – are you boy?" Five fingers as round and fat as sausages reached to pat the dog's head, but the creature shied away. Emma immediately noticed that it had difficulty in placing one of its front paws on the ground. Dropping her bags, she moved cautiously towards the animal. When it began to wag its tail and attempted to reach her, she slowly extended a hand to comfort it. With confidence, but still wary of an unknown dog, she stroked the creature's head while running her other hand down the leg and gently lifting it to inspect the paw. A tiny fragment of wooden splinter had sunk deep into the pad. Emma took a closer look and decided it was protruding just enough for her to get a grip on it with her nails. With a little assistance from one of the boys to hold the dog steady, she felt she could remove it.

"Could one of you hold on to his collar for me?" she asked the boys who had gathered around. A sixteen-year-old boy with a thin, grey face and lank, straw-coloured hair shuffled forward.

"Buster's *my dog*," he scowled. "What d'you think you're doing to him?"

Emma showed the boy the paw and explained she could probably remove the splinter. It was causing the poor thing unnecessary discomfort. The boy eyed her suspiciously; but she seemed very sure of herself, and he decided to do as she'd requested.

"Get a good grip on that collar, will you?" Emma advised him. Then, steeling herself, she held the paw firmly in one hand while she secured the splinter between the thumb and forefinger of her other hand. "I'm pulling it out – *now*!" she exclaimed.

Much to Emma's relief, all of the splinter came out with one attempt. As it left the fleshy pad, poor Buster yelped and immediately struggled to lick his paw. Emma produced a clean handkerchief from her pocket and dabbed at the oozing wound. As efficiently as was possible while squatting on the pavement of a busy street, surrounded by boys, she bound the hanky around the dog's paw.

The group of boys were dumbstruck. She had worked quickly and competently. Now she knelt comforting Buster, who seemed to have taken a liking to her. "Good, *brave* boy!" She praised him with affection, and he licked the side of her face.

"Well, would you *believe* it!" one of the

boys eventually uttered. "What are you – a vet or something?"

"No," replied Emma, getting to her feet. "But my father is, and, if Buster was my dog, I'd make sure my dad saw him as soon as possible. I've removed all the splinter, but there could be some infection in the pad. Walking on dirty pavements won't help it to heal."

The grey-faced boy who owned the dog shuffled from one foot to the other, stared down at the pavement and muttered, "Look, thanks." He sounded embarrassed. "He must have got that splinter this morning when we were walking on the wasteground. I just hadn't noticed. I'll take care of him now."

Emma looked concerned and persisted: "My dad's clinic is only a little way up the road. You really should bring Buster in for him to take a proper look at that paw. It could become a problem if it's not treated."

The boy continued to appear uncomfortable and failed to meet her gaze. He didn't like to be told what to do.

"Like I said – he'll be all right," he

repeated, and slouched off among the others. Buster stared after Emma, tugging on his lead as if he wanted to stay longer with her.

Emma looked at the dog's big, soft, brown eyes; they were so appealing. She sighed, picked up her bags, and carried on walking with what she hoped looked like confidence. But she soon became aware of the trickle of sweat running down her back, making her school blouse stick to her skin.

"*Why* do I do these things?" she mumbled to herself.